# Disney's
# THE GREAT
# MOUSE DETECTIVE

A GOLDEN BOOK · NEW YORK

Western Publishing Company, Inc., Racine, Wisconsin 53404

One rainy evening, Dr. David Q. Dawson, just back in London from years out of England, was looking for a place to stay. Hearing an odd noise coming from an alley, he went to investigate.

"Oh, my!" he said, seeing a sobbing girl. "Are you all right, my dear?"

The girl shook her head.

"Come now, dry those eyes," said Dawson, lending her his handkerchief. "Tell me what's troubling you."

"I'm lost," said the girl. "I'm trying to find the famous detective, Basil of Baker Street."

"There, there. I, uh, well, I don't know any Basil, but I do remember where Baker Street is. Just come with me. We'll find this chap together."

Dawson and the girl were let into Basil's flat by his housekeeper. While they were waiting for Basil to return, the door suddenly burst open and a fellow with a pistol raced into the room.

"Who are you?" Dawson asked, alarmed.

"Why, I am Basil of Baker Street."

"Mr. Basil, I need your help," said the girl.

"Not right now," said Basil. "I'm in the midst of chasing the most fiendish criminal in England!"

"But my daddy's gone," pleaded the girl.

Removing a disguise he was wearing, Basil said,
"I haven't time to look for lost fathers, Miss...uh..."

"Flaversham. Olivia Flaversham. And I didn't lose him.
He was taken by a bat."

"Did you say 'bat'?" asked Basil. "Did that bat have
a broken wing?"

"I don't know," said Olivia. "But he had a peg leg."

Suddenly Olivia screamed. A bat's face was peering in at the closed window. By the time they got outside, the bat was gone. But he had dropped his hat, and he had left a trail of peg-legged footprints.

"Wonderful!" said Basil. "That bat, one Fidget by name, is employed by the very fiend I was chasing."

"Why is that wonderful?" said Olivia. "He stole my daddy!"

"It is wonderful because"—and Basil puffed out his chest—"we now have the clues we need to find your father. And not only will we find him, but we will catch up with Fidget's employer, none other than the notorious Professor Ratigan. Why, at this very moment Ratigan may be plotting something unspeakable!"

Indeed he was. In his secret hideout near the river, Ratigan had assembled his gang of criminals.

"My friends," he said with a wicked grin. "We are getting ready for the most evil scheme of my entire career. We are going to pay a special visit to the palace to help our beloved Mouse Queen of England celebrate her fifty-year reign. It will be a night she'll never forget!"

"And," he continued in a boastful voice, "I'll finally be recognized as the greatest criminal mind of all time. Nothing can stand in my way—not even Basil of Baker Street!"

"Boo! Hiss!" shouted the gang members at the mention of Basil's name. Then they gave Ratigan a great big cheer.

Somebody else was at Ratigan's hideout, too, but not by choice. In a lonely prison cell sat Olivia's father, surrounded by doll parts and gears.

Suddenly the door opened and an unwelcome visitor popped his head in.

"Quite a scheme, eh, Flaversham?" said Ratigan. "And such an important part for a toymaker to play."

"The whole thing is monstrous," said Flaversham.
"Well, think what you may," sneered Ratigan. "But finish your job in time—or else!"
"Or else what?" Flaversham gulped.
"Just in case you have second thoughts, I've taken the liberty of having your daughter brought here."
"Not Olivia!"

Meanwhile, inside a dark toy store, Fidget was also getting ready for Ratigan's big night. He was busy stripping the uniforms off toy soldiers and stuffing them into a large sack.

Pulling out a list, he started to read: "Get the following ...tools, gears, girl...oh, I didn't get the girl...uniforms... I've got plenty of those."

Just then, Fidget heard a noise and saw something at the window. Basil had convinced Dawson to join him and Olivia on the search for her father. And with the help of their dog friend, Toby, they had tracked Fidget to the toy store.

"Gotta hide," said Fidget to himself, dropping the list.

In the toy store were hundreds of toys.

"Just remember," said Basil to Dawson, "Fidget may be hiding here. So be careful. And don't let Olivia out of your sight."

As they looked for clues, they noticed the dolls with missing uniforms and gears. Dawson also found the list Fidget had dropped. But before he could show it to Basil...

...the toy store came to life! Wind-up toys were marching at them from everywhere.

In the confusion, Fidget grabbed Olivia, popped her into a sack, and fled. Basil and Dawson were unable to stop him.

"Confound it," said Basil. "I told you to watch the girl. Oh, never mind, old chap," he continued, seeing that Dawson was upset. "We'll get her back."

Examining Fidget's list and discovering it had been soaked in river water, Basil figured it must have come from the riverfront. Disguised as sailors, he and Dawson were able to locate Ratigan's hideout.

In the darkness they were suddenly blinded by bright lights. A huge "Welcome, Basil" banner unfurled. And they were surrounded by Ratigan's gang yelling, "Surprise!"

"With your disguise, I would hardly know you…the greatest detective in all mousedom," said Ratigan with an evil laugh. "I'm so glad Fidget dropped that list. Otherwise I might have missed the pleasure of your company."

"Ratigan, I'll see you in jail yet," said Basil.

"You don't seem to understand…I've won!" said Ratigan, laughing even harder.

With Basil and Dawson tied to an elaborate trap, and Olivia corked up inside a bottle, Ratigan inspected the large package that held Flaversham's invention.

"Flaversham," he said, "let me congratulate you on a superb job. I'm sure the queen will be delighted with my gift."

Then Ratigan kissed his pet cat, Felicia. "Good-bye, my
little rosebud," he said. "Daddy will see you soon." And she
padded off toward the palace carrying Ratigan's gang on her
back. They were dressed in the uniforms from the toy
store, and ready to carry out Ratigan's evil plan.

To Basil and Dawson, Ratigan bid farewell. "It was my
fond hope to stay and witness your final scene," he said.
"But I cannot keep the queen waiting."

At the palace, the Mouse Queen of England was waiting
to address her subjects. Fidget appeared with a note: "To
our beloved queen this gift we send, as her fifty-year reign
comes to an end." And then the gift was unwrapped—a life-
size mechanical double of the queen!

"My goodness!" said the real queen with alarm as the
doll began to move. And then she fled...right into the arms
of Professor Ratigan!

With the real queen tied up, Flaversham was forced to imitate her voice as the mechanical queen doll addressed her subjects.

"On this occasion we are here to honor not only my fifty years as queen, but someone of truly noble stature. I present to you a statesman among mice, a gifted leader, a crusader for justice, freedom, and truth...and my new royal consort—Professor Ratigan!"

The audience drew back in horror and disbelief.

"Thank you, Your Majesty," said Ratigan. "Now I have a few suggestions for running the country.

"Item one...anyone who disagrees with me about anything will be gotten rid of...."

"...Item ninety-six," Ratigan continued. "There shall be a heavy tax against the elderly, the sick, and—especially—the little children."

"That's ridiculous!" shouted someone in the crowd.

"Perhaps I haven't made myself clear," Ratigan said.
"I have the power. This is my kingdom—of course, with
your permission, Your Majesty."

Meanwhile, Basil, Dawson, and Olivia had escaped from
Ratigan's den and arrived at the palace. Rushing onstage,
Basil shouted, "Arrest that fiend!"

Ratigan tried to escape, but Basil finally caught up with him and ended his life of crime. The queen honored Basil for his bravery and service to the crown.

Back at Baker Street, Olivia and her father bid Basil a thankful good-bye. But Dawson stayed on.

Although they had many cases together, Dawson always looked back with special fondness on that first one, his introduction to the most brilliant mouse he had ever known…Basil of Baker Street.